CARTER HIGH® MYSTERIES

DRAMA CLUB
Mystery

By Eleanor Robins

SADDLEBACK
EDUCATIONAL PUBLISHING

CARTER HIGH®
M Y S T E R I E S

SADDLEBACK
EDUCATIONAL PUBLISHING
www.sdlback.com

Copyright ©2006, 2011 by Saddleback Educational Publishing

ISBN-13: 978-1-61651-562-1
ISBN-10: 1-61651-562-7
eBook: 978-1-61247-130-3

Printed in Malaysia

20 19 18 17 16   5 6 7 8 9

Chapter 1

Logan was on the bus. The bus had just arrived at school. Logan got off the bus. Drake and Paige got off behind him.

All three were good friends. And they all lived at Grayson Apartments.

Logan said, "I need to go. See you both at lunch."

Drake said, "Good luck, Logan."

"Thanks," Logan said. "I'll need it."

"Why? Where are you going, Logan?" Paige asked.

"I'm going to Mrs. Scott's room," Logan said.

Mrs. Scott was an English teacher.

She also helped with the drama club.

"Why are you going to her room now?" Paige asked.

"The members of the drama club are meeting there. We're going to find out who'll be in the new play. I want to find out which part I got," Logan said.

"Do you still want the clown part?" Paige asked.

"Yeah," Logan said.

The play was about a clown. And the clown part was the best.

"Do you think you'll get the part?" Paige asked.

Logan said, "No. I think Kyle will get it. He's a good actor. He always gets the best part in all of the plays."

"Good luck. I hope you get it," Paige said.

"Thanks," Logan said.

"See you at lunch," Drake said.

Logan hurried into the school. And he went to Mrs. Scott's room.

Mrs. Scott said, "Hurry and get a seat, Logan. We don't have a lot of time. So we need to get started."

Logan was glad to see Brooke. He quickly sat down next to her.

Logan liked Brooke. He wanted to date her. But she dated Tucker. Tucker was in Logan's math class.

Logan hoped Brooke and Tucker broke up. So maybe Brooke would date him.

Mrs. Scott said, "I'll read all of your names. Then I'll tell you which part you got. Some of you will have back-up parts."

Logan was sure that he got a back-up part. He didn't think he would get a star part.

Mrs. Scott said, "Back-up parts are

also important. You have to be ready to go on if someone isn't here. So study your part. And learn it well."

Logan could hardly wait to find out who got to play the clown.

Mrs. Scott said, "Logan, you'll be the clown."

Logan couldn't believe it. He got the part he wanted. And it was the best part in the play.

Mrs. Scott said, "That will mean a lot of work for you, Logan. But I'm sure you can do it."

"Yes. I can do it," he said.

Then Mrs. Scott called Kyle's name. She said, "Kyle, you'll be the back-up for Logan."

Logan wished he could see Kyle's face. But he couldn't see Kyle.

Mrs. Scott said, "Brooke, you'll be the clown's wife."

Logan hoped Brooke would be the clown's wife. And he knew she wanted that part.

Mrs. Scott told the rest of the students what their parts would be. Then she talked about how they could help with the play.

Then Mrs. Scott said, "Time to go. I'll see you at rehearsal after school. Don't be late."

The students got up to go.

Kyle came over. He seemed mad.

Kyle said, "Mrs. Scott should've given that part to me, not you. I'm the best actor. And you know that."

Logan said, "Yeah, you're the best actor. But Mrs. Scott thinks I'm the best actor for this part."

"I don't think you are. And Mrs. Scott will find that out when we start to practice. And then she'll give the part to me," Kyle said.

"Don't count on it," Logan said.

Logan was going to work hard. He would show Kyle that he was the best one for the part, not Kyle.

Chapter 2

It was two weeks later. Logan was on his way to lunch. He'd just heard some very good news. Brooke and Tucker had broken up.

Logan went into the lunchroom. He saw Drake. Drake was sitting at a table.

Logan got his tray. Then he went over to the table. And he sat down with Drake.

Logan said, "I just heard some good news."

"What?" Drake asked.

"You know I want to date Brooke. I just heard that she and Tucker broke up. So I'm going to ask her for a date," Logan said.

"Are you sure that they broke up?" Drake asked.

"Three or four people told me they did," Logan said.

Drake said, "You better make sure before you ask Brooke for a date. You don't want to ask some other guy's girl for a date."

"Okay. I'll make sure before I ask her," Logan said. He would ask Tucker and make sure. He didn't want to ask Brooke.

Paige came over to the table. Jack and Lin were with her. They sat down at the table.

Then Willow came over, too.

They were all good friends. Jack and Lin rode the bus with Logan, Drake, and Paige. Willow rode a special bus. It had a wheelchair lift.

"Do you like the clown part, Logan?" Paige asked.

"Yeah," Logan said.

"I can't wait to see your play," Willow said.

"Me, too," Jack said.

"And me," Lin said.

Then all six started to talk about the new play. They ate lunch. And they talked. Then lunch was over.

Logan put his tray away. Then he started walking to math class.

Logan saw Tucker. Tucker was walking down the hall in front of him. Tucker was on his way to math class, too.

Logan said, "Wait, Tucker. I'll walk with you."

Logan wanted to ask Tucker about Brooke. He wanted to make sure they really had broken up.

Tucker stopped and waited for Logan.

Logan asked, "Did you and Brooke break up?"

Tucker seemed mad that Logan had asked him that.

"Yeah, I broke up with Brooke. Why do you want to know?" Tucker asked.

"I want to date her. Is that okay with you?" Logan said.

"Why should I care? I told you I broke up with her," Tucker said.

They got to math class. So the boys didn't say any more to each other. They hurried into the classroom. They were almost late.

Logan was glad Tucker broke up with Brooke. So it would be okay with Tucker for Logan to date her.

Logan worked hard in math class. But he was glad when class was over.

He hurried out to the hall. Tucker was right behind him.

Logan was looking for Brooke. Then he saw her. Logan hurried over to Brooke.

Logan said, "I heard you and Tucker broke up. How about going out on a date with me?"

"When?" Brooke asked.

"Friday night," Logan said.

"Sure. We can talk at rehearsal. But I have to get to class now, Logan," Brooke said.

"Okay," Logan said.

Things were going really well for Logan. He had the best part in the play. And he had a date with Brooke.

Chapter 3

It was Monday morning. Logan was glad. He was ready for the week to start. The play would start on Friday. And he could hardly wait to play the clown.

Logan got to the bus stop. He was early. Drake was also there.

Drake said, "I guess you're glad the play is this Friday."

"Yeah, I can hardly wait," Logan said.

"Your first play where you'll be the star. How does it feel to be the star?" Drake asked.

"Great," Logan said.

Logan really was the star. So he didn't think Drake was joking with him.

"Is Kyle still mad because you got the clown part?" Drake asked.

"I don't think so. He was at first. But he doesn't seem like he's mad now. He just wants the play to be good We need to sell a lot of tickets. Then we can raise enough money for another play," Logan said.

"I heard a lot people bought tickets," Drake said

Logan said, "I heard that, too. I don't know if it is true. But I sold all of my tickets."

Drake laughed. Then Drake said, "That doesn't surprise me. You made me buy one."

"I didn't make you buy one, dude," Logan said.

"Just joking," Drake said.

And Logan was sure Drake was joking.

Logan said, "We have to turn in the money at rehearsal today. Mrs. Scott will tell us then how many tickets are left. So I can tell you tomorrow how many were sold."

The boys just stood there for a few minutes. And they didn't talk.

Then Drake asked, "How did your date with Brooke go?"

"Great," Logan said.

"What did you do?" Drake asked.

"We went to a movie. And then we got something to eat," Logan said.

"Did you and Brooke see Tucker?" Drake asked.

Logan said, "Yeah, he was at the movie. And then we saw him when we went out to eat."

"Did he have a date?" Drake asked.

"I don't know. I don't think so," Logan said.

"Did Tucker talk to you and Brooke?" Drake asked.

"No. But I don't think he saw us," Logan said.

"What are your plans? Are you going to go out with Brooke again?" Drake asked.

"Yeah, we want to go out again this weekend. But we can't. We'll be too busy with the play," Logan said.

Some more kids came to the bus stop. So Logan and Drake didn't talk any more about the play or Logan's date.

Chapter 4

Logan was at rehearsal. The students had turned in their money.

Mrs. Scott said, "I can't believe it. You sold all of your tickets. And some of you want to sell more tickets. We might have to give the play an extra day."

Kyle said, "Great. Then we can have another play soon."

Mrs. Scott said, "It's time for rehearsal to start."

Mrs. Scott put the money in a box. She left the box in the room next to the stage. The box didn't have a lock.

Then Mrs. Scott and the students

went to the stage.

The students started to rehearse. They all wore their costumes. Logan wore his clown costume. He was the only one in a clown costume.

Mrs. Scott said, "You're doing a great job, Logan. Keep up the good work."

"Thanks, Mrs. Scott," Logan said.

Logan was on stage most of the time.

A few times Logan went out to get some water. And he had to go by the room where the money was kept.

The group practiced for a long time. But it didn't seem long to Logan.

Then Mrs. Scott said, "Time to stop for today."

Logan thought he did a good job. And Mrs. Scott said he did. Logan thought the others did a good job, too.

Mrs. Scott said, "All of you did a great job. See you tomorrow."

The students changed out of their costumes. Then they went home.

Logan wasn't at home long when the phone rang. It was Mrs. Scott.

"I need to see the drama club tomorrow. Come to my room before school. All of you have to be there," Mrs. Scott said.

"Is something wrong, Mrs. Scott?"

Mrs. Scott sounded very upset. Logan was sure something was very wrong.

"Someone took the ticket money during rehearsal. I found out after all of you left," Mrs. Scott said.

That surprised Logan very much.

"Who took the money, Mrs. Scott?" Logan asked.

Mrs. Scott said, "I don't know. I don't want to say this. But someone in the drama club must have taken it."

Logan said, "One of us? I don't believe that."

It couldn't have been one of them. They all cared too much about the play.

"Do you know who took the money?" Mrs. Scott asked.

"No," Logan said.

"Did you see someone near the money?" Mrs. Scott asked.

"No," Logan said.

"Did you go into the room where the money was?" Mrs. Scott asked.

"No," Logan said.

Why did Mrs. Scott ask him that?

"Are you sure?" Mrs. Scott asked.

Logan said, "Yes, Mrs. Scott. But why did you ask me if I'm sure?"

At first, Mrs. Scott didn't answer. Then she said, "Kyle saw someone in the room with the money. It was a person in a clown costume."

Logan was the only one who wore a clown costume. So Logan knew Mrs. Scott thought he'd taken the money.

But how could Mrs. Scott believe he took the money?

"Kyle is wrong. I didn't go into the room with the money. And I didn't take the money," Logan said.

"Kyle didn't say you took the money. He saw someone in a clown costume. He didn't say it was you. But someone took the money," Mrs. Scott said.

"It wasn't me," Logan said.

"I didn't say it was you, Logan," Mrs. Scott said.

But Mrs. Scott sounded like she thought Logan took the money.

"I told Mr. Glenn the money was gone," Mrs. Scott said. Mr. Glenn was the principal.

"Mr. Glenn called the police. The police will be at the meeting tomorrow. And they want to talk to all of you," Mrs. Scott said.

Logan thought he knew what Kyle would tell them. Kyle would tell them about the person in the clown costume.

"Be sure you're at the meeting, Logan," Mrs. Scott said.

"I will be," Logan said.

Logan didn't want to go to the meeting. But he knew he would have to go. He had to find out who took the ticket money.

Chapter 5

Logan called Drake.

Drake said, "I thought you might call. Were many tickets sold?"

"Yeah, but I didn't call to tell you that. I need to talk to you, Jack, Willow, Lin, and Paige," Logan said.

"When do you want to talk to us? Before school tomorrow? Or at lunch?" Drake asked.

"Now, in front of my apartment building," Logan said.

"Why now? What's wrong, Logan?" Drake asked.

"I'm in big trouble. Really big trouble," Logan said.

"What kind of trouble?" Drake asked. He sounded worried about Logan.

"I'll tell you when I see you. But hurry. I'm going to call the others now," Logan said.

Drake said, "You call Jack and Willow. And I'll tell Lin and Paige. We'll meet in front of your building as soon as we can."

"Thanks," Logan said.

Logan called Jack and Willow. He told them he needed to talk to them now. And he asked them to meet him in front of his building.

Then Logan hurried outside. It wasn't long until the other five friends arrived.

Drake said, "We're all here now, Logan. So tell us what's wrong. You don't look so good."

"That's for sure," Jack said.

"I'm in big trouble. Really big trouble," Logan said.

"What kind of trouble, Logan?" Paige asked.

"Someone stole the ticket money," Logan said. "And Mrs. Scott thinks I took it."

"Why does she think that, Logan?" Lin asked.

"Kyle said he saw someone in a clown costume near the money. And I was the only one in a clown costume," Logan said.

"Were you near the money, Logan?" Drake asked.

"No! And I didn't take the money," Logan said.

"We know you didn't take the money," Paige said.

"Kyle didn't say I took it. He just said

he saw someone in a clown costume near the money," Logan said.

"You were the only one in a clown costume. So it was the same thing," Drake said.

"Did someone else say they saw the person near the money?" Willow asked.

"I don't know. Mrs. Scott only said that Kyle did," Logan said.

"Maybe Kyle took the money. And he made up the story about the clown," Paige said.

"But why would he do that, Paige?" Logan asked.

"Maybe he said it so that you couldn't be in the play. And he could be the clown," Lin said.

"Yeah, so he could be the star. And not you," Drake said.

"Kyle took the money," Jack said.

"But it's okay with Kyle now. He was

mad at first. But he isn't now," Logan said.

"Maybe he's still mad. And you don't know he is," Drake said.

"Kyle took the money. For sure," Jack said.

Willow said, "You don't know that, Jack. So don't say for sure that he did."

"But he could have taken the money," Drake said.

Jack said, "That's for sure. What can I do to help, dude? Just say the word. And I'll do it."

Paige asked, "Who's in the drama club? We can call them for you, Logan. And we can ask them if they saw someone near the money. Then we can meet back here in about 30 minutes. And we can share what we find out."

"Good idea, Paige," Willow said.

"That sounds like a plan to me," Drake said.

Logan said, "It feels good to know you believe me. And that you'll all help me."

Logan felt a little better. Logan told his friends the names of the people in the drama club. Then they hurried off to call them.

Logan hoped his friends could find out something that would help him. They had to find out something. Or else he'd be in big trouble. Not just with the school but also with the police.

Chapter 6

A little later, Logan was in front of his building. Four of his friends were with him. He could hardly wait to hear what they'd found out. He hoped it was something that would help him.

Lin said, "Paige can't come, Logan. She has to help her mom. But she sent a text. She didn't find out anything that would help you."

"How about the rest of you? Did any of you find out where Kyle was? Could he have taken the ticket money?" Logan asked.

"He was with people the whole time. Three or four people told me that. So it couldn't have been him," Lin said.

"I heard the same," Jack said.

"So did I," Drake and Willow said.

"Did you find out anything that would help me?" Logan asked.

But Logan didn't think they did. They would have already told him if they had.

"No. Only bad news," Jack said.

"What?" Logan asked.

But Logan didn't want to hear more bad news. So he wasn't sure he wanted to know.

"Kyle wasn't the only one who saw the person in the clown costume near the money. Some others did, too. But they didn't tell Mrs. Scott," Drake said.

So Kyle didn't tell a lie just to get Logan in trouble.

"You're the only one with a clown costume. So they all think it was you," Jack said.

"But it wasn't me," Logan said.

"We know that," Willow said.

"Yeah, we do," Drake said.

But Logan knew that they were his friends. People who weren't his friends might not believe him.

"What am I going to do? I have to prove I didn't take the money. Or I'll be in big trouble with the school. And with the police," Logan said.

"Don't worry, Logan. We're going to help you," Willow said.

"Yes. We'll help you," Lin said.

Jack said, "What can I do to help?"

"Maybe you'll find out something at the meeting tomorrow morning, Logan. Something that will help you," Lin said.

"Yeah, maybe you will," Drake said.

But Logan didn't think he would.

Willow said, "We know Kyle didn't take the money. But maybe someone who was mad at you did. Can you think of someone who's mad at you?"

"No. Only someone who doesn't like me would do that. And I don't know anyone who doesn't like me. Do you?" Logan asked.

The other four looked down at the ground. No one said anything.

Logan said, "Don't all of you talk at the same time."

But no one talked.

"Someone answer my question. Do you know someone who doesn't like me?" Logan asked.

At first, no one said anything.

Then Jack said, "Yes."

"Who?" Logan asked.

"Too many to name," Jack said.

That surprised Logan very much.

"That wasn't nice, Jack. You shouldn't have said that," Willow said.

Logan said, "You can't name even one person, Jack."

At least Logan hoped Jack couldn't do that.

"Tucker," Jack said.

"Tucker? Why wouldn't Tucker like me? I didn't do anything to him," Logan said.

"It's because of Brooke," Jack said.

"Why?" Logan asked.

"Because you had a date with her," Jack said.

Logan said, "Tucker and Brooke broke up. So why would he care if I date her?"

"He still likes her. And he wants them to get back together," Jack said.

Logan said, "I don't believe that. He was the one who broke up with her."

"But it's true," Jack said.

Logan looked at Drake. He asked, "What about you, Drake? You know Tucker. Do you think that it's true?"

"Yeah, it's true. Tucker still likes Brooke. And he wants them to get back together. I thought you knew that," Drake said.

"I didn't. Is that why some other guys don't like me? Because I dated or tried to date their girls?" Logan asked.

"Yeah," Drake said.

"Maybe Tucker did take the money. Or maybe some other guy who doesn't like me took it. But how can I prove that?" Logan asked.

Chapter 7

For a few minutes, his friends didn't answer. But they were all thinking about what they could do to help Logan.

Then Lin said, "I have an idea."

"What?" the other four asked at the same time.

"Where did Mrs. Scott get the clown costume, Logan? Do you know?" Lin asked.

"She got it at a store on Cramer Street," Logan said.

"Maybe someone else bought a costume like your costume," Lin said.

"And then wore it to steal the money," Drake said.

Lin said, "So this is my idea. We could go to the store. And we could talk to the owner. And maybe we'll find out someone else bought a clown costume. One that's just like your costume, Logan."

"That sounds like a plan to me," Drake said.

Jack said, "Just say the word. And I'll take you there."

Jack was the only one of them who had a car. So he was always glad to take them somewhere.

"Can you take us tomorrow after school, Jack?" Drake asked.

"Can do," Jack said.

"But that might be, too late, dude," Logan said.

"Why?" Drake asked.

"The police will be at the meeting tomorrow morning. I need to find out something to help me before then," Logan said.

Willow said, "Maybe we can go now, Logan. Do you think the store is still open?"

Logan said, "Wait. I'll call 411 from my cell. Then I'll connect to the store."

Drake said, "Good idea. Then we'll know if it's open now."

Logan dialed. Four-one-one automatically dialed the store.

A man answered.

Logan was glad to know the store was still open.

Logan asked, "What time does the store close?"

The man told Logan when the costume store closed.

"What did you find out, Logan?" Drake asked.

"The store is still open. But only for an hour," Logan said.

Lin said, "Good. We still have time to go over there. And maybe we can find out something to help you."

"I think this is a good idea. But we have to tell our parents before we go," Willow said. "It's almost dinner."

"Yeah, we'd better do that, Willow," Logan said.

"But we need to hurry," Drake said.

"Meet back here in ten minutes. Then we can go. Is that okay with you, Jack?" Lin said.

"Okay with me," Jack said.

"Thanks for the help," Logan said.

"Don't thank us yet, Logan. Wait until we find out who really took the money," Willow said.

"Because we'll find out," Drake said.

Logan hoped Drake was right. But he wasn't sure they would find out who took the money.

But they just had to find out. Or Logan would be in very big trouble.

Chapter 8

Logan went inside to tell his parents. Then he hurried back outside. He couldn't wait to go to the costume store.

Logan walked over to Jack's car. Jack sat in the car. Drake and Lin were standing next to it.

Willow wheeled up to them. She had their school yearbook. It was the one from last year.

Willow said, "My mom said I can't go. She said I need to study."

Willow handed the yearbook to Logan. "Take this with you," she said. "You might need to show the owner a picture of Tucker. Or a picture of someone else."

"Good idea. Thanks," Logan said.

"I'm sorry I can't go with you," Willow said.

"That's okay, Willow. You brought the yearbook. And we didn't think about that. So you've been a big help," Logan said.

Willow said, "Text me what you find out."

"We will," Lin said.

Then Logan, Drake, and Lin got into the car with Jack.

Jack said, "Just say the word. And we'll be on our way."

"Go," Logan said.

They drove off.

It didn't take long to get to the costume store. But it seemed like a long time to Logan.

Soon, Jack parked his car.

Then Jack said, "I might have to move

my car. So I'll wait here."

"Okay," Logan said.

Then Logan, Drake, and Lin went into the costume store. Lin had the yearbook with her.

A man came over to them. The man said, "My name is Mr. Chen. Can I help you find something?"

Lin said, "No thanks. We're just looking right now."

Mr. Chen walked to the other side of the store.

Drake said, "Logan, you look for a clown costume like yours. And then we'll ask if someone else bought it."

"Okay," Logan said. Logan started to look at the costumes.

It didn't take Logan long to find one like his. He took it over to Mr. Chen.

Logan asked, "Did someone buy a clown costume like this?"

"Maybe in the last few days," Drake said.

Mr. Chen said, "Yes. A couple of days ago. A boy about your age bought it from me."

"Did he say why he wanted a costume just like this?" Drake asked.

Mr. Chen said, "Yes. He needed it for a play at the high school. He said he has a costume like this. But he got a lot of paint on it. Now it doesn't look good. So he wanted a new one. So it would look good for the play."

Drake said, "You were right, Lin."

Lin opened the yearbook. She turned to a page with a picture of Tucker. It had pictures of a lot of other students, too. She showed the yearbook to Mr. Chen.

Lin said, "Please look at this page. Do you see a picture of the boy?"

Mr. Chen looked at the pictures. Then he pointed to the picture of Tucker.

Mr. Chen said, "This is the boy."

"Are you sure?" Logan asked.

"Yes, I'm sure. But why do you want to know?" Mr. Chen asked.

Logan said, "The boy got me into a lot of trouble. Now I'll be able to get out of trouble. Thank you very much, Mr. Chen."

Logan wasn't the only one with a clown costume. Tucker had one, too. But Tucker didn't have a good reason to buy the costume. And Tucker had wanted one just like the one Logan had.

Now Logan wanted to go to the meeting tomorrow. And he could hardly wait to get there. He was sure everything would be okay now.